HOW TO WRITE A NOVEL

MERCY O.R

ISBN 979-888546510-6

The Book Is Dedicated To All My Friends, Family, Parents, And Almighty. Special Thanks To All the Reviewers, Designers, and Technical Teams. For Whom This Entire Book Can Be Possible.

♡♡♡

Contents

Foreword

This book is foreword to all mentor and authors and Professor Sanjay Rout for the amazing mentoring and guideance for success this project.The book is Published by ISL Publications, India. All rights reserved. Any unauthorized reprint or use of this material is prohibited. No part of this book may be reproduced or transmitted in any form or by any means, electronic or mechanical, including photocopying, recording, or by any information storage and retrieval system without express wrote permission from the author/publisher. Please do not participate in or encourage piracy of copyrighted materials in violation of the author's rights. Purchase only authorized editions.

Preface

This book is an effort to all authors specially new authors who are passionate into writing novel. This book is a bibel to reach the target for full filling the book writing aspirations.

ÞÞÞ

Acknowledgements

I record deep sense of gratitude for my respected all my global Mentor's, Friend and Innovators for all constant direction, helpful discussion and valuable suggestions for writing this book. Due to his valuable suggestions and regular encouragement. I would be able to complete this work and fulfillment of my dream. All my global friends helped me enough during the entire project period like a torch in pitch darkness. I shall remain highly indebted to all throughout my life.

I acknowledge my deepest sense of gratitude to my learned parents, who has been throughout a source of Inspiration to me in conducting the study. Who helped me at various stages of the study directly or indirectly. He also enlightened me to follow the path of duty.

Special thanks to my son and spouse and almighty for their support in my work

Prologue

The book is all about how to writing a novel. It has given all steps which will help everyone to wite novel and fiction books.

ᑭᑭᑭ

ONE

CHAPTER-I

This chapter focuses mainly on the things you must know before writing a novel, below is the thing you must study before writing a novel. Firstly, focus on your tense and grammar.

Sentence formation

There are twenty-six letters language alphabet which includes:

A B C D E F G H I J K L M N O P Q R S T U V W X Y Z

When these letters come together it become "word";

A word is a combination of two or more alphabet.

Example,

A+T=AT

W+A+S=WAS

And so on. We have three letter word, four word etc .

When two or more word comes together it become phrase.

What is a phrase?, A phrase is a group of words without a finite verb.

What is a verb?, Verb is an action words or doing words.

***Example* of a phrase are;**

In the bush

The man
On the table
And so on... ...

This phrase cannot stand on its own except it is attached to another part of sentence before it can make real sense.

A clause can be defined as a group of words that as a subject and a finite verb. There are two main types of clause:Main clause and subordinate clause. Main clause can stand on its own and it is otherwise known as independent clause (e.g He jogs every morning.). Main clause is also equivalent to a simple sentence. Subordinate clause is known as dependent clause because it cannot stand on its own and make meaning until it is attached to the main clause. For example:" before I left", "where there is no traffic".

Hence, a sentence can be made up of both main clause and subordinate clause(s).

Example:

Sentence (with two clauses): I saw the man (main clause) before I left (subordinate clause) because I wanted to give him something (subordinate clause).

Sentence (with two sentences): (Mary jogs every morning (main clause) where there is no traffic (subordinate clause).

A sentence can be define as a group of words, phrase and clause and as a complete meaning. hus, a complete sentence must have at least a minimum of three things: A subject, been and object. The subject is typically a noun of a person. And , if there's a subject there's a bound to be a "verb" because all verb need a subject. Finally, the object of a sentence is the thing that's being acted open the subject.

Subject-verb-object

In linguistic typology, subject-verb-object is a sentence structure where the subject comes first, the verb second and the object third. The subject is the actor of sentence, the person or thing doing the action. The verb is the doing words , the action of the sentence. The object is the element of the sentence that is acted on, that the verb is directed towards.

Example.

I drove the car yesterday.

"I" is the subject, "drove" is the verb and "the car yesterday" is the object.

Thus, Subject; who/what the sentence is about

Verb; what the subject does/is

Object; a person or things that is affected by the action of a verb.

Subject verb agreement

What is verb agreement?

To say that a verb agrees in form with it's subject is to say that a verb has more than one form and that each form matches up with a particular kind of subject. Here are three common examples.

Singular

I live, you live, he lives, she lives

Plural

We live, you live, they live

To write a standard English correctly, you need to know which form goes with each types of subject. Where to find the subject In a clause or whether the subject is singular or plural.

Making Verb agree with subject

In most cases,the subject affects the form of the verb only when the verb is in the present tense. Except for the verb "BE" and for subjunctive verb form the rules of agreement in the present tense are as follows:

[1] with the third-person singular, add "s" of "es" to the bare form of the verb. Eg;

She works at the market

He polishes his shoe once in a week.

Exception: the verb "have" will become "has"

Example;

Everyone has moments of self doubt

Uncertainty has gripped all of us.

Rules of Concord

Concord in Grammar means the agreement between the subject and the verb or the agreement between a verb/ predicate and other element of clause structure. In the use of Concord rules in English language, there are 24 rules of Concord. There are:

<Rule one>

Subject and Verb Concord

When the subject in a sentence is singular the verb must be singular and when the subject in a sentence is plural the verb must be plural.

Example 1

"She" [singular subject] gose [singular verb], not ; she go.

Example 2

"The girl " [plural subject] "go" [plural verb]

Thus, singular subject must go with singular verb, plural subject must go with plural verb.

Rule 2

When everybody or everyone is used , the object must be singular not plural.

Example;

Everybody knows his or her name

Not everyday knows there name

Rule 3

When prayer, suggestion, wish, demand, recommend or resolution is used in a sentence, the verb that follow must be plural. Whether the subject is singular or plural.

Example

{1} It has been suggested that he go, not goes .

{2} The board has recommend that the manager resign, not resigns.

Rule 4

The principal of proximity

The principal state that when there is a list of nouns or pronouns at the level of the subject, it is the nearest noun or pronoun to the position of the verb that will determine the choice of the verb.

Example

If Roland fails his examination, his teacher, his parents his friends or Roland is to be blame. [Four different people]

Rule 5

When "many" is used, the verb and the noun that follow must be singular

Example.

[1] many a candidate [not candidates] "speak" [not speaks] bad English.

[2] many a girl [not girls] is [not are] here.

Rule 6

Indefinite pronoun Concord

When any of the following words are used, singular verb should be used. Such words are; everybody, everything, everyone, everywhere, nobody, nothing,no one, nowhere, someone, something, somebody, anyone, anything, anybody anywhere and each. The next verb should be singular.

Example

(1) nothing goes [not go]

(2) Everybody thinks [not think]

Rule 7

When who, whose, which and that refer to a previously mentioned noun or pronoun, such noun or pronoun is a relative noun.

Example

One of the farmers who plant (not plants) on the farm has (not have) been asked to withdraw.

Rule 8

Uncountable Noun of Concord

Uncountable Noun are the noun that cannot be counted eg water , information etc. Note; all uncountable nouns will add "S" at the back.

Example.

(1) the police work hard (not works) but, that policdman (not policemen) works (not work) hard

Note; police is a collective noun that is why it attract a plural verb.

But policeman is a singular noun, hence a singular verb.

Rule 9

Plural Tantums

Plural Tantums are nouns that came in plural forms. Some of these words have final "S", while some do not. However, whenever any of the following forms appear it must be followed by a singular verb.

[1] School Subject; Economics, mathematics, physics etc. You can see that all of the words end with "S" but it does not show plurality.

[2] Games; Drafts, snakes and ladders etc. all end with "S" but do not show plurality.

Example;

The series of incident makes (not make) me shudder.

Note: there are some nouns that don't appear as singular at all but as plurals they often attract plural verb.

Such words are; founds, annals, spirits, surroundings, guts etc. All these nouns not verb cannot appear without "S" and hence they attract plural verbs.

Example

[1] The remains [corpse] of the boy have [not has] been berried.

Rule 10

When two Subject are joined together by "and" but the two Subject refers to only one person or thing, a singular verb should be used.

Example

Our principal and English language teacher knows me.

In the above sentence, our principal and English language teacher is not two different people. But , our principal and our English language teacher. Hence, the Subject is our principal and it is a singular Noun. Hence, singular verb.

Consider this example

Our principal and the English language teacher

Rule 11

Coordinating Concord

When two Subject are joined together by "and" the verb to be used should be plural.

Example

Robert and Michelle are here (not is)

Rule 12

When a collective Noun denoting category not a collective noun is used , the verb to be used should be in plural form.

Example

The weak are (not is) left to their faith

The poor need help (not helps or needs)

Rule 13

When amount or unit is mentioned in a statement, units such as five thousand, ten thousand, twenty meters, five times etc. The next verb must be singular.

Example

Two pounds of flour is (not are) here

Rule 14

Mathematical facts

When mathematical facts are used such as addition, subtraction, division etc . are used , the verb will be any of singular and plural. That is, a singular verb can be used when mathematical facts are used.

Example

(1)Ten plus ten is or are twenty

(2)five mutiplied by ten is or are fifty

Rule 15

When every precedes a plural the next verb is plural

Example

(1)Every ten litter of oil brought come (not comes) with a bonus of an extra liter

But when every appears without a plural number, the verb to be used is singular.

Example

(1) Every men and women speaks (not speak) English language here.

Rule 16

When "must" is used the verb will either be singular or plural depending on weather the referent is a countable or uncountable Noun

Example

Much of the water has (not have) been spllied

Rule 17

When "All" appears, it means either everything or all the people. When all means everything, the verb to be used should be singular be when all means all people, the verb to be use should be plural.

Example

(1) All are already seated in the hall. In the above sentence, "All" means all the people all the people are already seated in the hall, hence a plural verb. BUT "All is well with me"

In the above sentence, "All" means everything is well with me hence a singular verb.

Example

All about John are (not is) on the bus. That means , only is absent.

Rule 18

When either or neither joins two singular nouns together the following verb should be singular.

Example

(1) Either John or Jackson knows me

(2) Neither John nor her friend was here

But when either or neither John two Subject (one singular and other plural) , the verb should be choosen by considering the nearer of the two Subject

Example

Either James or his friend knows me.

You can see that the word "friends" is nearer to the verb gap than it is near James.

This rule also apply when "But or even " join two Subject.

Example

Not only Akpos but even teacher laugh at me .

Rule 19

When each appears in a Concord. a singular noun plus a singular verb will be chosen

Example

(1) Each boy (not boys) has a car. But when "each of or when of" appear, the next noun should be plural but next verb should be singular.

Example

Each of the candidates (not candidate) stands (not Stand) a good stand to win a scholarship.

Rule 20

When a pair of is used, the verb must be singular

Example

A pair of trousers (not trouser) lies (not lie) on the bed

Rule 21

National Concord

National Concord is also called collective noun Concord. A collective noun is a noun that stand for many unit that constitute that singular word. E.g

Club; is a collective noun for members.so we can say; members of this association.

Example

Our club meet (not meets) ones in a week

However, in some situation. A singular verb goes with a collective noun, here is the principal.

*If the collective noun performs an action, a plural verb follows but if not a singular verb follows.

Example 1

Our club is celebrating it's twentieth anniversary today.in the above sentence, you can see that "our club" perform no action. Hence, a singular verb is used. But;

Example 2

Our club are (not is) going on a vacation tomorrow.

You can see that the above sentence is different from each other's . Here the club is performing the action "going" hence, we will use a plural verb "Are" compliance with a rule.

Rule 22

Parenthesis

The parenthesis statement is an additional statement to what has already been said before.

Note; A parenthetical statement should be concerned in choosing the verb that will follow.

Example

The teacher, not the student is (not are) in the class

Rule 23

When any of these following are used. The Subject of the clause would be the noun and pronoun that comes before the marker of accompliment. Words like as mush as, together with, not less than, in association with, including, like etc.

Example

Marry, as well as her friends "is" (not are) beautiful.

The answer is "IS" because Mary is the noun that comes before as well as.hence, marry is the Subject and it's a singular noun hence a singular verb..

Rule 24

When more than is used , the word or number that comes after "more than" will determine the next verb.

Example

(1)more than five mangoes (not are) here.

Do not think more than one means at least two that you will use a plural verb.

TWO

CHAPTER-II

DEFINITION OF LITERATURE

The word literature is derived from the word "literates" (meaning) able to read and write. In this sense, literature can be used to describe all printed materials which give instructions, information etc.

Literature can also be defined as a creative or imaginative work or art produce by poetry, drama and prose.

BRIFE HISTORY OF LITERATURE

The beginning of literature itself in all societies is basically oral, where people chant songs. For instance, at the community gatherings, social occasions or events etc. This is usually done with lyrical qualities which purely express themselves and pass from generation to generation in the oral forms. Stories and folklores were usually preserved in the memory of people through generations.

Thus, the primitive level of literature was in the oral forms before the Advent of the art of writing. When the development of writing came, the development of literature in visible nationalist forms. The Art of writing tends to make literature materials(otherwise having a tendency of getting lost early) to be long lasting when preserved in black and white. Written literature are therefore be seen as the embodiment of literature in written form either handwriting or printed.

PPP

THREE

CHAPTER-III

Genres of literature

Literature has three major facets namely. Poetry,drama and prose. These facets often referred to literary genres. Thus; here we will consentrat on how to write a prose.

Genre; this is a term used in literary criticism to designate the distinct category into which literary works grouped according to form techniques or sometimes Subject matter.

FOUR

CHAPTER-IV

A Poetry

Poetry has to do with the act of poem writing. Poem can be described as a literary composition characterized by the presence of imagination, emotion, Truth, sense of impression and concrete language expressed rhythmically and with an orderly arrangements of parts and possessing within itself a unity.

Types of poetry

- Lyrical poem
- Naration poem
- Ballard
- Epic
- Lullaby
- Elegy/Dirge
- Pastoral poem
- Dramatic poem

- Sonnet
- Epitaph

ϸϸϸ

FIVE

CHAPTER-V

Image

Drama

Drama is a genre of literature which creates or recreates human experience through "acting" it's the representing of human action.

forms of Drama

1. **Comedy**: this is a form of drama aims to create joy of laughter

2. **Tragedy**: this is the opposite of comedy, it is a drama whose atmosphere is often serious and tensed with an unhappy ending.
3. **Tragedy-comedy:** it is a play thtat combines both elements of tragedy and comedy.

Some others forms of Drama are:

- Farce
- Melodrama
- Closed drama
- Realistic
- Mine/pantomime

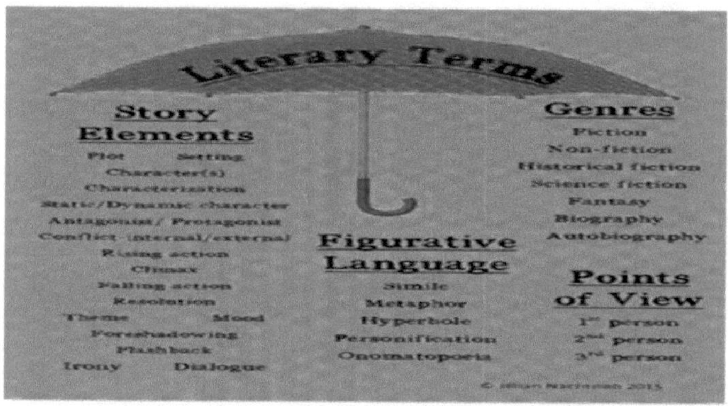

Image

ᑭᑭᑭ

SIX

CHAPTER-VI

Literary Terms

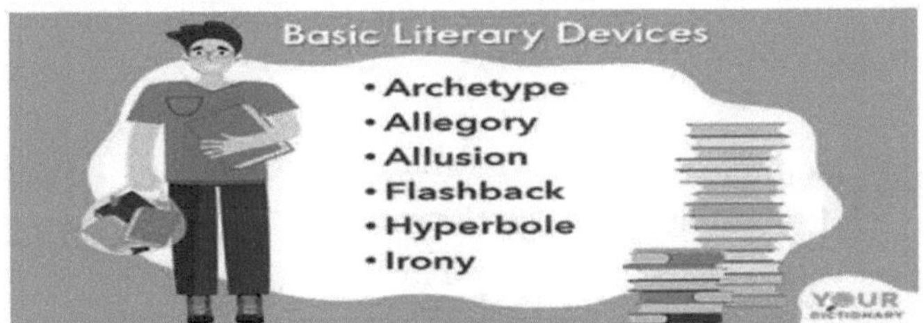

Image

1. **Stanza:** in a poetry we have what is called stanza, a poem is usually written in decisions of stanza.

- **Monomer**: A line stanza.

- **Couplet**: a two line stanza
- **Triplet**: a three line stanza
- **Quatrain**: a four line stanza
- **Quintets**: a five line stanza
- **Sestet:** a six line stanza
- **Septet**: a seven line stanza
- **Octave** : a eight line stanza

v. **Rhythm**: this is the precise flow of material movement between sound and events. It most essentially synchronized with sound and through a good rhymic pattern, a song like effect is usually achieved

v. **Mood/Tone**: This is the state of mind of the author when making its composition. It reflect the feelings of the writer which the readers cannot feel except through the words of the work.

v. **Rhyme**: This is correspondence in sound on word-endings. It usually at the end of the poetry lines. Rhyme is much of a poetic device whereby the final sound of words are similar

   - Example
   - He stumbled through the gate
   - When I was having my date
   - He couldn't believe that I was awake

v. **Imagery**: in the literary sense, it means the collection of images within a literary work or a unity of a literary work. Imagery in literature could be based upon the physical state of the setting in which yeh work is produced and thus presenting present word heavy laden with meaning.

v. **Allegory**: This is an extended metaphor in which object, persons and action in a narrative either in prose or verse are equated with meaning that lies outside the narrative itself

v. **Satire**: satire is a term used for a literary manner bleading a critical attitude with humor and for the purpose of improving human institution or humanity

v. **Flashback**: This is a narrative technique used by a novelist or playwright to present in a particular character.

v. **Dilemma**: This is a short story told to teach a moral lesson. It is often told with animal representing human.

v. **Metre**: metre occur when a person voice goes up or down at regular intervals in pronunciation of words.

v. **Ballad**: This is a short poem often handed down from generation to generation. This means that it's largest part is preserved through memory, it has themes celebrating legends and great heroes.

v. **Settings**: This is the physical periodic background in which a particular work of literature was written.

v. **Dialogue**: This deal with the exchanging of words between two or more character in a peace of writing

v. **Plot** : This is the arrangements of events in a work of Art. It simply indicate the sequential manner in which one event leads to another.

v. **Theme**: This is the pre-occupation of the written. It simply revele what the writer is intended to write.

v. **Prologue/Epilogue**: prologue is a preface to a work of Art. It is the introduction speach made at the beginning of a text

v. **Allusion**: this is a reference to something outside the immediate scope of what is being presented. It may be reference to characters or events in history mythology and works of literature

v. **Romance**: this is s story written either in verse or prose about wild and improbable adventures. The story could also be about nature. Example, love in the summer by mercy.
v. **Monologue**: it is a long speach by an actor, when a character speak all by himself and some of his words are actually addressed to some absent fellow characters.
v. **Conflict**: it refers to the disagreement between two or more character.
v. **Protagonist**: he is the main character in a novel
v. **Antagonist**: he/she oppose protagonist through out the story
v. **Resolution**: this is the resolution of the dramatic conflict immediately after the climax in a play

v. : it means that the readers knows something that one or more characters in a piece of drama are not aware of
v. **Suspens**: it is the state of anxiety and expectation in the readers of a play or novel
v. **Soliloquy**: it is a device in a drama or novel which allows a character to engage in a loud self talk for the readers to have assess to what is on his/her mind .
v. **Asisde** : this term refers to a speach by the character directed to the audience to the exclusion of fellow characters in drama.
v. **Climax**: this refers to a point in dramatic presentation when the progression of events reaches a moment of consummation.
v. **Audition**: This reefers to a theater practice in which actors of a play are selected to play specific assigned roles in the performance

v. **Flashback**: it's a dramatic or literary technics which entails a recall of what had happened before

Prologue: it is the formal introduction to a play written in prose or verse whose content is relevant to the unfolding events in the play.

SEVEN

CHAPTER-VII

Image

Prose

The term prose applies to all forms of written or spoken expression which do not have a regular rhythmic pattern. Prose can be divided into fiction and non fiction.

- **Fiction**: this is the term used for narrative writing drawn from the imagination of the author rather than history or fact. The term is usually associated with novels and stories, though drama and narative poetry are also forms of fiction.

  Examples of fiction are

1. Novel
2. Epistolary
3. Novelette
4. Emotive prose.
5. Scientific prose etc.

- **Non fiction**

This is the opposite of fiction, it deals with the true experience and happenings. Non fiction means prose writings that deals with a fact. Example of non fiction are.

1. Biography
2. Auto biography

Element of prose

- **Story or Subject matter:** Any work of art which is classified as prose must have a story that it tells or a subject matter that revolves around which is the kernel of the work that is presented to the readers to interpret or decipher. The story consist of those major event or incident in the work which help in facilitating a concise summary of the work of art.

- **Plot**: The plot of awork of prose refers to the way and manner in which the events or incident narrated in the work and arranged. There are two types of plot structure which a writer can used in the presentation of the story. The first type of plot structure is called linear or chronological or organic plot structure.

Thus, the plot of a story is the 'what' of the story . It is the story line , the rendering of events in a story from the beginning to end. A writer can choose to maximize the ordering of the story line to achieve some special emotional or historical effect as the case may be. The plot consist basically of actions or stimulus and reaction or response to action. Starting out with the initiation event, it progresses to the rising action, conflict, climax and then the resolution. In the common parlance we will say that a story has a beginning, middle and an end.

- **Linear/Chronology/Organic plot** : in a narration with a linear, chronology or organic plot structure, the story commences from the beginning and there is a gradual movement in chronological order to the end of the story being narrated. Thus, every work of art with a linear plot structure will have a beginning, a middle and an end which give it form.

At the beginning, the readers get to know some of the principal character and the problem which need to be resolved. In the middle of , the storyline become interesting and complicated and an attempt is made to sustain the readers interest with only the relevant facts while the ending provideds the resolution of the problem. The ending may not satisfy the readers. However, it would be such that it would be able to make the reder use in it's different fact.

- **Inorganic or Episodic plot:** In writing a work of art, the writers may decided to write in a non chronological order. For instance, in many detective novels, or shot stories the narrator often start when a crime has been committed which there after necessitates the involvement of a detective to solve. In such novel, the order narration dose follow a chronological order or pattern. An illustration of what we meet by a chronological or non Chronological order of narration is "appreciate" at this stage. However, the writer can alter the narrative sequence and began the story through the use of flashback technique as one of the character recounts his experience on that fateful day.

This is an example of non-chronological plot structure which are not usually thightly knitted together. In this kind of scenario, part of the story can be removed completely and being recounted would still be understood by the readers. Plot development involves the use of conflict to characters to move the story forward.

- **Plot organization:**

- **Types of plot organization**

1. **Exposition**: This is the introductory stage when the major characters and events are exposed or presented to the readers.
2. **Complication**: This is the stage when the events, situation and occurrences in the work become more complicated, new characters and incident are

introduced which help in making the storyline more complex. It is the beginning of raising action.

3. **Climax**: This is the stage when the greatest Crises or position in work occurs
4. **Anti climax**: At this point in the narrating of story, the issues which have engendered a crisis are not as potent as before and there is a leasning of the heightened action
5. **Resolution**: This is the stage when the different issues raised in the course of the narration are resolved.

- **Tools for plot development**

1. **Suspense**: This entails the deliberate withholding of information by the written in an attempt to heighten and sustain the readers interest in the story information which is Germaine to the resolution of the conflict is not received by the writer and this helps in making the plot structure more complex and mysterious.
2. **Foreshadowing or prefiguration**: prefiguration occurs in a work of art when the writer present certain event which predict other events that would occur as the story develop. Usually, the first event is very minor and might not even be noticed by a readers. However, the Minor event would serve as a clue that provides an inkling as to the reasons why a more major events occurs.
3. **Digression**: in developing the plot of a work of art, the writer might digresss from the main storyline by creating a story within a story which is know as digression. In such an instance, the flashback technique through which the character bring to the present events from the past becomes very effective.

- **Character**

Every work of prose must have a character whose action, inactions and interactions help in facilitating the development of the storyline. They act out the event recounted by the author and characters can represent human being, inanimate object animals etc.

- **Types of character**

1. **Hero/Heroin/Protagonist**: The protagonist of the story is also the central or major character of the story. He is the person around whom the storyline revolves his/her intention with other characters help the readers to have an understanding of what the story entails.
2. **Anti hero/Antagonist/Antiheroine**: This is a major character whose action are greared toward undermining the protagonist of the story. The antagonist does the exact opposite of what the protagonist dose. Most of times he/she embodies evel qualities.
3. **Eponymous character**: This is a major character whose name is also the source of the title of the narrative.
4. **Flat character**: flat character is unreceptive to redical personality change and it is relatively easy for the reader to predict his or her action.
5. **Round character**: The round character who is also called dynamic character possesses the quality of unpredictability or an ability to change , to turn from evel to good and vice-versa. The description of in-depth in an attempt by the writer to present a full picture of his/her personality

- **Characterisation**

In creating characters writers are expected to have in-depth knowledge of their creation. Some authorities in the literary sphere have described the creative writer as a god who possesses the power to to kill man, wealth and long life on the characters provided he or she is logical in the way this is done. When a writer has created a character,there are different methods through which the writer has presented the characters and which assist the reader to have a good understanding of the personality of each figure. One of the method of making characters come to life in the mind of the readers is through the provision of a physical description of the characters.

A writer may also provide information about the character through his/her way of speaking, walking manners and how he interact with people. With this dramatic method of providing information, the readers decides the kind of personality the character has. A writer can also use one character to provide information about another character as gleaned from the characters physical description and actions as well as from comments provided by other characters and by the narrator of the events being recounted.

Technique of characterization

There are different techniques which can be used by the writer to facilitate the process of characterization. The three basic approaches are naming, showing or telling.

1. Naming: This is a simple method by which the name of the character gives the readers an inkling of his/her personality, physique, qualities etc. The name which might be allegorical or descriptive, series as a basis for a graphic re-creation of who the character is in the mind of the reder. The names can also be allusion to names

of prominent historical personalities through whom the readers is expected to have an idea of the personality of the character.

2. Showing: The technique of characterization include the use of action. It is dramatic and through the things that the character talks about or the way he or she talks, walk or act. The readers is able to decipher his or her personality.
3. Telling: This method comes to the fore when the author/ narrator of a character provides information about a particular character. Most often the information that is provided through this means can serve as a concise account or summary of the personality of character and what he/she embodies. Information can also be provided by the third person or ominscient narrator on a character through a portrayal of the character's thought and the things which go through his/her mind.

Point of view

This refers to the position or perspective from which the story being narrated is presented to the readers. There are two major methods of doing this. These are; the first person's narrative techniques and the ominscient narrative techniques. It should be noted that there is also a third person's point of view.

1. First person narrative techniques: This technique is employed when the story is narrated through one of the characters. The character narrates the story through the fist person's point of view and he goes by the designation "I". The voice of the narrator disappears the readers because he believes that he is telling a story of which he already has an in-depth knowledge, sees the narrator as

credile. There is an element of intimacy associated with a fist person narrator.

2. Third person/Omniscient point of view: The narrator in a narrative where the third person or Omniscient point of view is used is an outsider as he is not a character in the story being narrated. However, the narrator possesses the ability to know everything that happens in the story. He can even present the thought of a character to the reader. He passes comments on the characters for the benefit of the reader. It also allows room for authorial intrusion.
3. Third person object point of view: with this narrative techniques, the narrator's or authors personal comments about event, situation and personality are deliberately excluded. The narrator dose not present information on material sourced form the thought or mind of the character. The reader has the opportunity to form his own independent opinion about each character. It often involves a lot of dialogue and it is difficult for the reader to know the thoughts of the character since the reader is only limited to external information drawn from one character's interaction with other characters.

Setting

Setting can be defined as the physical it social environment within which the character in a work of prose operate. There are different methods which a writer can use to provide information about the setting of a story. The fist method is through pictorial representation. This entails an almost lifelike description of events, situations and characters in a way that enables the readers to have a graphic idea of the spectacle being described. Another approach is called the impressionistic approach. Here, the writer attempt to evoke feelings in the readers about the setting of character being described in order to pass a message across. At times, with this kind of approach, figure of speech otherwise called figurative it metaphorical language, become very useful.

In analysing the setting of a story, there are many things which the readers as the interpret of the text has to put into consideration. They include the physical environment of the story, the social environment of the story encompasses the town, neighbourhood or geographical location within which or around which the story is situated. In respect of social setting, this revolves around the language, culture and social condition within which the character operate and how they interact with one another. Setting is important in the creatio of a work of art because of the interrelationship which exist between it and the writers thematic preoccupation as well as the characters whose action life to the writer's ideas.

Them

A them can be defined as an issue of life, which a writer discuss or highlight in a work of art. In a prose work, it is possible to have several isses of life which form the bedrock of the writer's focus. There issue of life might revoked around corruption, Power, love death etc.

The theme of a story is the "way" of the story. When any writer picks up his pen to write, he has a message in his mind he intends to pass across. That very message is the theme of the story. It is also referred as the moral of a story.

Diction

In passing his/her Message in a work of art, the writer makes use of diction, which encompasses the words. Phrases and sentence that are stung together to make a cohesive and understandable whole. Diction in a work of art may possesses the quality of being formal, informal, figurative or allusive. There are times when in the course of narration, the writer use diction to establish different between characters to highlight there social or economic status, there level or illiteracy as well as their personalities.

Symbol

A symbol is a narrative technique useb by a writer to pass a information at different stages of the narration. A symbol can represent itself and something. For example, red and black represent theses colours, while at the symbolic level, they represent love/danger or death. Writers usually place symbols in strategic locations in the narration, including the title. In prose, literature, many writers make use of traditional or archetypal symbols to enhance the quality of the work. Traditional symbols are symbols to which particular meanings have been associated over times such as the colour "white" representing peace and purity and the rose flower symbolizing love. Archetypal symbols are derived from myths, legend, folk tales and religion.

EIGHT

CHAPTER-VIII

Satire

It is a literary convention in prose literature through which a writer, critical of certain aspects of society highlight issues through the depiction of the flaws, faults and mistakes of the characters. A work of prose fiction that is satirical makes use of humor, which is intended to make the reader laugh at the mistakes of the character but at the same time think of constructive methods that can be employed to correct such mistake. In highlighting such mistakes, the writer make use of exaggeration. The exaggeration portrayal of the weakness of the character helps to foreground the message of the writer.

How to write a novel everything you need to know

Things you must do before writing a novel

Before you start writing a novel, here are some steps you need to follow. The more you prepare yourself before started writing a novel the better you are while writing.

v. Nail down the story ideal
v. Read book in your genre
v. Chose your book's point of view

v. Establish the settings
v. Develop your character
v. Establish the conflict and stakes
v. Create an outline
v. Chose your story structure
v. Pick a writer software
v. Write to market
v. Establish a writing routine
v. Consider literary devices and techniques
v. Revise your story
v. Work with other readers

v. Hire a professional editor.

- **Nail down the story ideal**

An obvious step, but not an easy step one to class off. In fact, you might find yourself making up other first tasks to avoid naming this one. Such as finding the perfect writing spot, buying the perfect stationary set and doing other shorter forms of creative writing. While all of these thing might help you on your way to writing a novel without spending time really solidifying what you want to write about this novel to be simply won't come to fruition.

- **Read books in your genre**

"I can't write without a reader it's precisely like a kiss .... You can't do it alone" if you want your novel to be attractive to propective readers. You need to first understand how to think like a reader. And the way to do that is to *"let all say it together;"* Read!. The question there was that "if you don't like reading books why would you want to write then?.

There are many reasons why you you must read other novels as aspiring author:

- You will have an understanding of what's already been done by other authors so you can focus on how to create something new.
- You will also have an understanding of what has proven popular in a given genre, you'll know what expectations readers have so that you can determine how to write a story that will sertify them.
- And lastly, reading other story will improve your reading skills and also give you ability to learn new things.

- **Chose your book point of view**

Choosing your book point of view in a very important aspect while writing a novel because extremely important step in starting your novel. You know how?, When gossip moves through the grapevine, it tends to stray further and further from the Truth as it passes from person to person. This is because any time a person tells a story, they invitably add their own unique biases, thoughts and perspective. For this reason, choosing the point of view your novel will be told from an extremely important step in starting your novel and will have a huge impact on the actual story itself.

Here are the different things you might want to consider:

i. First person narrative techniques: The story is told from the perspective of the writing or fictional narrator. The main pronoun use is "I"

ii. Second person narrative techniques: The readers is addressed directly and ask them to put them selfs in your shoes of a character. The main pronoun used is "You"
iii. Third person's narrative techniques: The narrator is all knowing and can revel anything that is happening to any character at any point in the story. The pronoun used are third person limited.

- **Establish the settings**

Consider this line from pride and prejudice; "what are men to rock and mountain?" .

This line guilds smoothly from the page when Elizabeth Bennett takes a trip to the peak district in Georgian Era England. If, on the other hand, the book took place in modern day texes and a 20 years old Elizabeth Bennett spoke thumb words it would stick out like a sore thumb.The key here is context, and context or settings of a story will dictate everything about it from character to plot to conflict and beyond.

If you are planning to write about a settings outside your own immediate knowledge, make sure you do adequate research. Consider working with sensitive readers if you are writing about a place or culture outside your own.

- **Develop your main character**

It is very important for an author to picture what their character looks like, starting from the inside and working your way out out is a better approach. Here are what you should work on;

- The goal: what dose your character want?. E.g, Harry petter's goal is to defeat Lord Voldemort.
- The motivation: why dose your character have this goal. Harry must defeat Lord Voldemort to ensure the wizarding world's safty and to venge his muderd parents.
- Static of Dynamic: will your character undergo fundamental changes throughout the course of the story or will reamin largely the same.

Once you have those core elements mention above, you can start exploring other aspects of your character using these resources.

- Create a character profile
- Look into your character's past
- Give your character the perfect name .

- **Establish the conflict and stakes.**

The conflict is what we make your character's part to achieving or not achieving. Their goal interesting to readers it's the sum total of obstacles the protagonist encounters along the way . In novels, there are two bored categories of conflict these are;

1. Internal conflict: what kinds of character flaws will hider the protagonist while they strive for their goal. For example, frode's internal conflict in the Lord of the rings was to let the ring corrupt him.
2. External conflict: what kind of circumstances and abstract outside of the protagonist control will prevent them from achieving their goals. Savron has made the

read to mount doom and the destruction of the ring near impossible.

- **Create an outlet**

In the world of fiction writing, there is often said to be two kinds of writers; ploter and pantsers. Plottar as you might have guessed plan where there novel will go before the start writing while pantsers will usually have a general idea of how their story will unfold, but will just down and write without doing ant initial outlet.

If your goal is writing and publishing a novel, we are suggested that you should follow the way of the ploter and create an outlet . There are countless ways of outlining a story but few most essential will be mentioned below;

a. Mind map: create a graph or some kind of usual representation of your plot points, characters, themes, conflict and chapters.
b. The skoletop: just make note on the key plot point. Think of it as a roadmap with only big name destination. How to get there is up to you

- **Choose your structure**

Choose the best and suitable structure for your story. Your story must have a good starting, middle and end. You can drastically change how readers perceive your story by altering how your structure you story.

- **Decide how to write your novel**

In this case, it doesn't mean that you are going to be a plotter or pantsers or how to work up the motivation to keep going. But literally how are you going to write your novel!. With pen and paper?, On word document?. Just do your research and pick the best one for yourself.

- **Write to market.**

After writing your novel, the next thing is to look for a publisher to publish your novel. If you are looking for a publisher both online and reel life publisher, kindly Message me via WhatsApp on +234 7062864132 or maill me@ mercyor74@gmail.com

- **Establish a writing routine**

We won't talk much about the important of this step, we all know that to make progress on any kind of goal working on it must become our regular routine.

- **Consider literary devices and techniques.**

There are countless literary devise that authors use while writing there novels... Some of them as been mentioned above.

- **Work with better readers**

Readers is something who read a manuscript before it's published, with the sole purpose of giving the authors feedback from a readers point of view.

- **Revise your story**

Editing your own story is not one-time deal because each time you read your story you will likely endup rewriting some parts which will require another read through, which might lead to more writing etc. To ensure you don't get caught in an endless cycle of editing don't edit everything once. Go through your novel looking for a specific issues and fix only those you can.

- **Hire a professional editor**

One of the most important parts of getting a novel ready for publication is to hire an editor. It might not be the cheapest investment but when you think of the many hours you've spent getting your novel to this point, the cost of getting an expert to perfect your story is likely worth it.

Kindly Message me now for your novel editing at an avoidable price;

What'app on; +234 7062864132

Email; mercyor74@gmail.com

NINE

CHAPTER-IX

How to write a novel

Written by ManDark.

Image

To write a good novel first thing that you should think about is your book start and it's ending because if you are starting a novel just by the thought of "Let the end be" believe me you are going to abandon it in the middle beacuse of lack of interest.

#2: Second thing is your plot, I have seen nowdays many writers make a plot in which they define their story completely. It really save readers time to read your book. So say no to plot details. Don't open everything that is going to happen in book.

#3: Next thing is "Suspence" If your book doesn't hold suspence then it will not catch the eye of the readers.

#4: Don't make it too long." Now days many writers are giving so much details on single person room and furtniture. They can write 1k word over it which really break the interest of a reader. I personally don't like so much details myself.

#5 " Happy ending is the heart taker. " You can write so much sad scenes in the book but people like happy endings. Write on crime, violence or anything but give a happy ending. They will love it.

Pen Name: ManDark

About the Author

ManDark otherwise known as Sara was an author from Pakistan, she wrote over 32 books. She is a house wife and still wanted to be an author. She is so passionate and hard working by fulfilling her dreams of being an author and still giving her imaginations the true colours. Right now she was writing on different platforms. On libri, she is writing book After Dark and on Kongfu books she was writing "Mend my heart, The king for escort, Dark Doors" etc.

To learn more about how to write a novel and other genres like action story, mysterious etc kindly message me via WhatsApp to join our whatsapp group chat +234 7062864132

About Author

Author : Mercy O.R

MERCY O.R Also known as Olanrewaju Rahamon Mercy is from Osun State
Nigeria. He was born on the 25th of June 2001, he attended geometry international
college in 2013 and graduated in 2016 after writing his junior certificate examination
(junior waec) . He further in his Education at Minaret college located in Nigeria, he graduated in
2019 and wrote his final year examination. He passes the exam and further is
education in university.

About Publisher

ISL Publications

ISL Publication is a Global firm working on Research Development, Advisory, Think-tank, Policy Research, Innovation Development, Publication, Legal, Media, Consulting, Coaching, Technology, Academic, Social Development, Communication, Firm working on various Future Business solutions.

Printed by Libri Plureos GmbH in Hamburg, Germany